EPIC FACTS FOR CURIOUS KIDS

1,000+ Fun and Interesting Facts for Smart Kids and Their Families

JOHN M. HOWELLS

Introduction

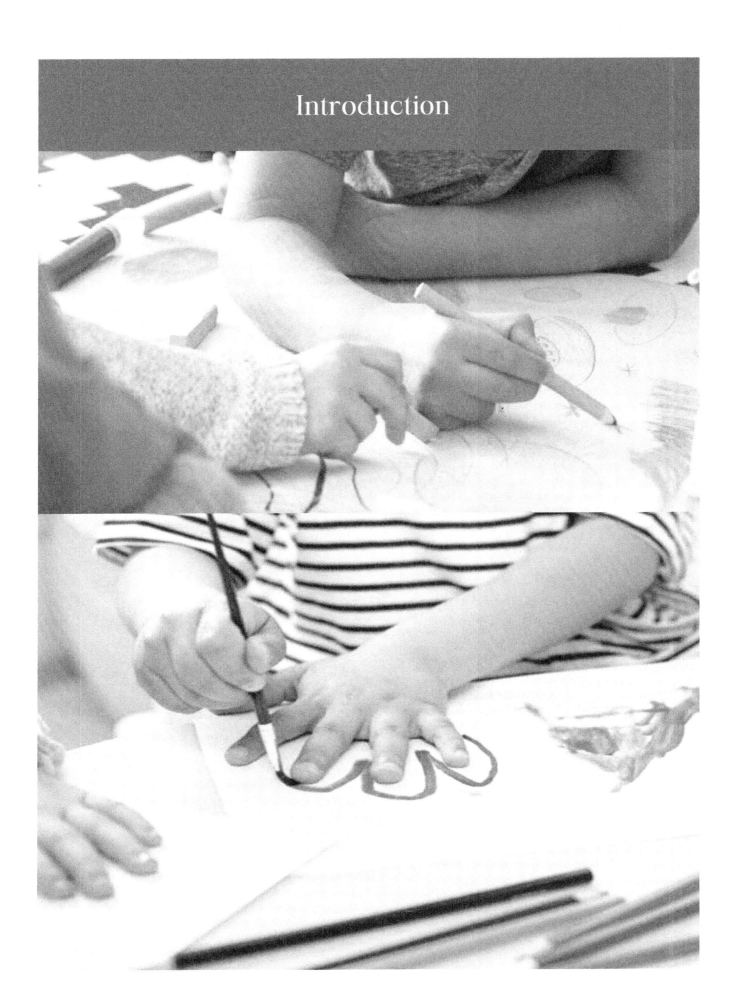

Have you ever wondered; how curious your child's young mind can be about the world around them? They are always observing random things and thinking random facts. And this thinking process can be highly crucial for child development. Knowing random stuff. and gaining general knowledge can lead to a holistic approach to life. And it can help in many ways, unknowingly, in your life.

Learning and gaining information are the only ways to train your brain. Reading practices and knowing random facts will enhance the learning process and help your brain evolve progressively. It will also develop intellectual curiosity, and the person will. become an active learner rather than a passive learner. And this trait will open up a myriad of opportunities for that person in life. Knowing facts can help you grow as a person and make you confident. Because when you start up a conversation with any p.erson and know many facts about that, it will help you connect more socially. Current trends, the geographical status of any country, scientific knowledge, or information on any other topic will create possibilities for you to grow socially.

Other than that, having a conscience about the tribulations faced by great personalities in life to achieve the eminence they attained by reading about them will surely inspire a person to strive for greatness. Learning can also increase your comprehensio.n skills and problem-solving skills. It will evolve cognitive skills necessary for personal development and especially for child development. For a child, it is even more important to know facts, for it will increase their interest in the world around the.m and they will also have the upper hand over their peers. It will develop learning habits and make them diligent and passionate about many things. Also, it increases creativity. A study shows that people who have general knowledge and known facts are mor.e creative than those who don't. So, gaining general knowledge and developing that habit is very important for any person, especially kids. There is a polish proverb stating:

"Gain knowledge, because knowledge is the key to power."

So, nourish the young minds with random fun facts about the development of human civilization, mind-blowing innovations, and amazing scientific facts about the species of flora and fauna on planet earth. This book is the best option if you're looking for .something for your child to read as it contains 1000 random facts about different attractions for your child. This book includes facts about the following things:

- Historical Facts
- Facts about human civilization development
- Geographical Facts
- Facts about great men in history
- Facts about the human body
- Scientific Facts
- Animal Facts
- Plant Facts
- Facts about great inventions in history
- Random Fun Facts

And so much more

This book provides an excellent opportunity for the kids to develop their intellectual ability and gain a wide range of information. It also solves parents' problems finding just the right reading material for their child. This book is not only meant for .children, but adults can also benefit from it and increase their knowledge. This is the best way to develop your brain and expand your knowledge in a fun and captivating way. This book will develop the following virtues in your child:

- Observation skills
- Curiosity
- Devotion
- Intellectual skills
- Knowledge
- Reading Habits

So, what are you waiting for? Get ready to feed the young minds and prepare to learn along the way.

01 The first building to have more than 100 floors was the Empire State Building.

02 The most visited city in the world is Bangkok, with twenty million people in 2018, followed by London and Paris.

03 Humans only make up 48% of users on the Internet. The other 52% of web traffic are bots.

04 The average human attention span has almost halved since 2000, decreasing from twenty seconds to twelve in 2018.

05 The oldest recorded tree in the world is reported to be 9,550 years old located in Dalarna, Sweden.

06 The oldest living system ever recorded is the Cyanobacterias, a type of bacteria that originated 2.8 billion years ago.

07 Being hungry causes serotonin levels to drop, causing a whirlwind of uncontrollable emotions including anxiety, stress and anger.

08 In Japan, it's considered to be good luck if a sumo-wrestler makes your baby cry.

09 Carrots used to be purple in color.

10 Over 99% of all species equating to five billion species in total that ever been on Earth have died out.

11 Jeff Bezos, the owner of Amazon.com., is also the owner of the Washington Post.

12 Google rents goats to replace lawn mowers at their Mountain View headquarters.

13 When you get blackout drunk, you don't actually forget anything because your brain wasn't recording in the first place.

14 Chaology is the study of chaos or chaos theory.

15 Male puppies will let female puppies win when they play, even though they are physically more powerful to encourage them to play more.

16 Before the renaissance era, three quarters of all books in the world were in Chinese.

17 The human eye can see a candle flickering up to thirty miles (forty eight kilometers) away on a dark night.

18 Due to a genetic mutation, the first blue eyed humans only began to appear six to ten thousand years ago.

19 For less than the cost of a Ferrari you can buy a renovated Boeing 737.

20 There are approximately 250,000 active patents applicable to the smartphone.

21 Astronauts would weigh one sixth of their weight if they were in space compared to on Earth.

22 If two rats were left alone in an enclosed area with enough room, they can multiply to a million within eighteen months.

23 It's impossible to taste food without saliva. This is because chemicals from the food must first dissolve in saliva. Once dissolved chemicals can be detected by receptors on taste buds.

24 The heaviest drinkers in the world are in Belarus with 17.5 liters consumed per capita every year.

25 Polar bears evolved from brown bears somewhere in the vicinity of Britain and Ireland 150,000 years ago.

There are more living organisms in a teaspoon of soil than there are humans in the world.

26

27

Oranges are not even in the top ten list of common foods when it comes to vitamin C levels.

There are 100 to 400 billion stars in the Milky Way, and more than 100 billion galaxies in the Universe.

28

29

The average person has 10,000 taste buds which are replaced every two weeks.

If all the stored batteries in the world were used for consumption, they would be flat in ten minutes.

30

31

The Filipino flag is flown with its red stripe up in times of war and blue side up in times of peace.

License plates in the Canadian Northwest territories are shaped like polar bears.

32

33

Crows have the ability to recognize human faces and even hold grudges against the ones they don't like.

In Mexico, artists like painters, sculptors and graphic artists can pay their taxes by donating pieces of artwork that they create to the government.

34

35

Apples float on water!

The stickers that you find on fruit are actually made of edible paper and the glue used to stick them on is actually food grade so even if you eat one, you'll be completely fine. **36**

37 When ants die they secrete a chemical that tells other ants to move the body to a sort of burial ground. If this chemical is sprayed on a live ant, other ants will treat it as a dead ant, regardless of what it does.

A cockroach can live up to several weeks without its head. It only dies due to hunger. **38**

39 Humans can only live without oxygen for three minutes, water for three days and food for three weeks.

An elephant drinks thirty four gallons (130 liters) of water a day. **40**

41 If you wear headphones for an hour, it will increase the amount of bacteria you have in your ear by 700 times.

Camels have three eyelids that protects them from the rough winds in deserts. **42**

43 Due to the placement of a donkey's eyes, it can see all four of its feet at all times.

Slugs have tentacles, blowholes, and thousands of teeth. **44**

45 In praying mantises 25% of all sexual encounters result in the death of the male as the female begins by ripping the male's head off.

It takes twelve bees a lifetime of work to create a teaspoon of honey. 46

47 There used to be horse sized ducks called "dromornithidae" roaming around present day Australia 50,000 years ago.

The fear of being away from your phone is called nomophobia. 48

49 Adding sugar to a wound will greatly reduce the pain and speed up the healing process.

Real diamonds don't show up in x-rays. 50

51 Germany was the first country to realise the link between smoking and lung cancer. .

52 Diet soda ruins your tooth enamel just as badly as cocaine and methamphetamines.

53 The Okinawa island in Japan has over four hundred people living above the age of 100 and is known as the healthiest place on earth.

54 The dot over the "j" or "i" is called a "tittle.".

55 Atelophobia is the fear of not being good enough or having imperfections.

56 The letter "u" was first used as a substitute for the word "you" by William Shakespeare in his comedy Love's Labour's Lost around 1595.

57 The actor who plays Mr. Bean, Rowan Atkinson, once saved a plane from crashing after the pilot passed out, despite never having piloted a plane before.

58 In order to drink, giraffes have to spread their almost 6.5 feet (two meter) long legs apart just to get close enough to the water.

59 The offspring of two identical sets of twins are legally cousins but genetically siblings.

60 Ryan Gosling was cast for the role of Noah in the movie "The Notebook" because the director wanted someone "not handsome."

61 When Charles Darwin first discovered the huge tortoises on the Galapagos Islands, he tried to ride them.

62 Crocodiles can not stick out their tongues or chew.

63 Marvel Comics once created a superhero named Thor who was a frog that had the power of Thor and is in a group called the "Pet Avengers."

64 The largest natural bridge in the world is the Ferry Bridge in China and was virtually unknown to the rest of the world until it was observed on Google Maps.

65 It took a whole month for Erno Rubik, the inventor of the Rubik's cube, to solve his own creation.

66 If you removed all the empty space from the atoms that make every human on Earth, all humans on Earth could fit into an apple.

67 If we somehow discovered a way to extract gold from the Earth's core, we would be able to cover all the land in gold up to our knees.

68 It rains diamonds on the planets Uranus and Neptune.

69 A blue whale can consume 480 million calories of food in a single dive.

70 There are only two parts on the human body that never stop growing, the ears and the nose.

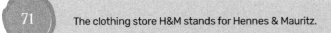

71 The clothing store H&M stands for Hennes & Mauritz.

72 We know more about the surface of the moon than we do about our own oceans.

73 The word "chec kilometersate" in chess comes from the Arabic "Shah Mat," which means the king is dead.

74 Voldemort in French translates to "flight of death."

75 Russia and Japan have still not signed a peace treaty to end World War Two.

76 Potatoes have more chromosomes than a human.

77 You can create 170,000 pencils from the average tree.

78 90% of Earth's ice is in Antarctica.

79 In Italy, the richest business is the mafia that turns over $178 billion a year, which is 7% of the country's GDP.

80 The words Tokyo, Beijing, and Seoul all translate to "capital" in English.

81 The sound you hear when you put a seashell next to your ear isn't the sea but the blood running through your veins.

82 The information travelling inside your brain is moving at 268 miles per hour (430 kilometers per hour).

83 In 1936, the Russians created a computer that ran on water.

84 Indonesia has more than 17,000 islands.

85 Mandarin is the most spoken language in the world with 1.1 billion speakers.

86 Diamonds are actually not that rare. A company called "De Beers" owns 95% of the market and suppresses supply to keep the prices high.

87 Over 50% of the oxygen supply we breathe comes from the Amazon rainforest.

88 A bus can replace forty cars if people made the switch.

89 The first web page went live on August 6, 1991, and was dedicated to information.

90 Zenography is the study of the planet Jupiter.

91 Although the Holy Bible is available for free at many places of worship, it is the most stolen book in the world.

92 In the early bottles, Coca-Cola contained cocaine.

93 You're not allowed to take mercury onto a commercial passenger plane as it can damage the aluminium the plane is made out of.

94 If you put an apple in the sea, it will float because it's less dense than seawater.

95 A newborn baby has about one cup of blood in their entire body.

DID YOU KNOW?

A HIPPO CAN FIT A 4-FOOT-TALL CHILD IN ITS OPEN MOUTH.

96 Big Ben in London is not the tower but the bell inside.

97 As a person dies, his or her hearing is the last sense to go.

98 Pirates used to wear eye patches on one eye during the day so they could see better at night with that same eye.

99 Astatine is the most rare element on earth with only thirty grams total in the earth's crust.

100 The most powerful organism is the Gonorrhea bacteria which can pull up to 100,000 times their size.

101 Humans have twenty three pairs of chromosomes while great apes have twenty four.

102 The Queen of England legally owns one third of the Earth's surface.

103 Amazon is the first company to ever hit a trillion dollars.

104 The highest divorce rate in the world by country is Luxembourg at 87%. The lowest is India with 1%.

105 Cats have been around since 3600 B.C.

106 A penguin has the ability to jump six feet (1.8 meters) out of the water with no aid.

107 Cuba has the highest doctor to patient ratio in the world.

108 300 hours of video are uploaded to YouTube every minute and almost five billion videos are watched on Youtube every single day.

109 There is a spa in India that is dedicated for elephants.

110 The average strawberry has 200 seeds on the outside. It's also not considered a fruit.

111 Hitler planned on invading Switzerland but gave in as it was too difficult with the surrounding mountains.

112 A group of ferrets is called a business.

113 During the Cold War, the US's passcode to nuclear missiles was eight zeroes so they could fire them as quick as possible.

114 Only 0.1% of an atom is matter. The rest is air.

115 There are over four million apps available for download on both the Android and Apple app store.

116 There are now twenty two countries worldwide that have no army, navy, or airforce.

117 There is an ancient book called "The Voynich" from the Italian Renaissance that no one can read.

118 In Cambodia, they sell "Happy Pizza" which is a cheese pizza garnished with weed on top.

119 Snoop Dogg has a book published named Rolling Words that has lyrics of all his songs that you can later rip out and use as rolling papers.

120 Jellyfish and lobsters are biologically immortal.

121 International "have a bad day" day is November 19th.

122 The human brain cell, the universe, and the Internet all have similar structures.

123 Sea otters hold hands when they sleep so they don't drift away from each other.

124 It's estimated that the world's helium supply will run out within the next twenty to thirty years.

125 The Pallas's cat is the oldest living species of modern cat that first appeared twelve million years ago.

Anuptaphobia is the fear of either remaining unmarried or marrying the wrong person. 126

127 Ostriches have eyes bigger than their heads.

The scent that lingers after it rains is called "petrichor.". 128

129 There are now digital pens that can record everything you write, draw or sketch on any surface.

More than half of the world's population is under the age of thirty. 130

131 2520 and twenty is the smallest number that can be divided by all numbers between one and ten.

The Maldive coconut is the largest growing seed in the world. 132

133 In one night, a mole can dig a tunnel 300 feet (one kilometer) long in soil.

You would be a few centimeters taller in space due to gravity. 134

135 If you were to take out someone's lungs and flatten it out, it would have the same surface area as one half of a tennis court.

Elephants are constantly tip toeing around. This is because the back of their foot has no bone and is all fat. 136

137 An octopus has nine brains, blue blood, and three hearts.

Polar bears hair is actually clear and it's the light they reflect that makes them appear to look white. 138

139 A chameleon can move its eyes two different directions at the same time.

There is a method of art called "tree shaping" where living trees are manipulated to create forms of art. 140

141 The average person will fall asleep in just seven minutes.

The majority of lipsticks contain fish scales. 142

143 Ischaemic heart disease and stroke are the world's biggest killers. Ischaemic means an inadequate blood supply to an organ.

The world's largest gold bar is 551 pounds (250 kilograms). 144

145 The fear of clowns is called "coulrophobia.".

There is a hole in the ozone layer sitting right above Antarctica that is twice the size of Europe. 146

147 Snails can sleep for up to three years.

The average shark has fifteen rows of teeth in each jaw. They can replace a tooth in a single day and lose over 30,000 teeth in their lifetime. 148

149 Fifty nine days on Earth is the equivalent of one on Mercury.

About 700 grapes go into one bottle of wine. 150

151 Hippos sweat the color red because it contains a pigment that acts as a natural sunscreen.

152 Cows methane creates just as much pollution as cars do.

153 Most of the dust you'll find in your house will be your dead skin.

154 The Great Barrier Reef is thought to be around 20 million years old

155 Backpfeifengesicht is a German word that means a face that badly needs a punch.

156 The cheapest gas prices in the world belong to Venezuela at just over a penny a liter.

157 In London, there's a public toilet encased in a glass cube that's made entirely of one-way glass where you can see passersby, but they can't see you.

158 The well known Leonardo da Vinci was a huge lover of animals. In fact, he was a vegetarian and was also known to buy birds from markets only to set them free.

159 Sternutaphobia is the fear of sneezing.

160 If you inhale a pea it is possible to sprout and grow in your lungs.

161 There's a lake in Western Australia called "Lake Hillier" that has water that's naturally pink.

162 The "Orca," also known as the killer whale, is actually from the dolphin family.

163 The Appian Way in Rome is a road that was built in 312 B.C. that is still used to this day.

164 Cherophobia is the fear of being happy or joyful with the expectation that something bad will happen.

165 Deltiology is the collection and study of picture postcards.

166 Justin Timberlake's mother was Ryan Gosling's legal guardian when he was a child.

167 Macklemore once worked at a juvenile detention center to help detainees express themselves by writing and creating rap lyrics.

168 One of the iTunes user agreement policies explicitly states that you're not allowed to use the program to build nuclear, chemical, or biological weapons.

169 A group of stingrays is called a fever.

170 Contrary to popular belief, white spots on fingernails are not a sign of a deficiency of calcium, zinc, or other vitamins in the diet. They're actually called "leukonychia," are completely harmless and are most commonly caused by minor injuries that occur. while the nail is growing.

171 Since Venus is not tilted on an axis like Earth, it experiences no seasons.

172 If an astronaut got out of his space suit on the moon, he would explode before he suffocated.

173 Earth is the only planet not named after a god.

174 There's a building in London called the "Walkie Talkie Building" that's shaped in such a way that it reflects sunlight like a giant magnifying glass, literally melting cars on the street below.

175 Almonds are members of the peach family.

The average tree is made up of about 1% of living cells at any given time. 176

177 Humans are not appropriate prey for great white sharks because their digestion is too slow to cope with the ratio of bone to muscle and fat.

A study conducted by the University of Oxford found that for every person that you fall in love with and accommodate into your life, you lose two close friends. 178

179 There's a travel agency in Tokyo called "Unagi Travel," who for a fee, will take your stuffed animal on vacation around the world.

Around 95% of the oceans have never been explored by mankind. 180

181 Your ears never stop growing during your entire lifetime.

Antarctica is the largest desert in the world, which may come as a surprise due to it being cold not hot. 182

183 The largest organ in the human body is the skin which makes up around 15% of our total body weight.

The longest mountain range on the planet is under the sea which is 10 times longer than the Andes . 184

185 More than two-thirds of the Earth's surface is covered by Oceans.

The Greeks invented the first democracy, which lasted only 185 years. **186**

187 The moon is around a quarter of the size of Earth.

While humans have been on Earth for around 2.5 million years so far, dinosaurs inhabited the planet for around 160 million years. **188**

189 Canada has the longest coastline on Earth.

We can only ever see up to 60% of the moon's surface at any one time. **190**

191 Some of the largest herbivore dinosaurs ate up to one ton of food every day, equivalent to a bus-sized pile of vegetables for a human.

The criteria for a piece of land to be considered a desert is that it loses more moisture than it gains. **192**

193 There are almost 38 million different sandwich combinations at Subway.

Since the beginning of mankind, it is estimated that around 45 billion people have died of malaria transmitted from mosquito bites. That is around half the human population that has ever lived. **194**

195 The Sahara Desert is currently in a dry period that will not last forever – it is predicted to be green and full of vegetation within the next 15,000 years, as it has been previously.

DID YOU KNOW ?

Malaria is considered to be responsible for the deaths of about half of all people who have ever lived.

The gravitational effect of the moon is what causes the rise and fall of sea tides on Earth. **196**

197 The first oranges were not orange, they were green.

Cows have four stomachs. **198**

199 The current American flag was designed by a high school student in 1958.

According to NASA, there were active volcanoes on the moon which would have been visible from Earth when dinosaurs inhabited the planet. **200**

201 Cleopatra originated from Greece, not Egypt.

202 In 1893, the US Supreme Court ruled that the tomato must be considered a vegetable, even though it is botanically a fruit.

203 Hawaii is the only US archipelago state.

204 The fastest animal in the world is the peregrine falcon.

205 Scotland has 421 different words for 'snow'.

206 The city of London has more than 8 million residents, speaking around 300 different languages.

207 Kleenex tissues were originally intended to be used for gas masks during the cotton shortages of World War One.

208 The tiny pocket in jeans was originally designed to store pocket watches.

209 The famous author Mark Twain invented the bra clasp.

210 Turkeys blush when they are scared or excited.

211 Starlings sing notes too high for humans to hear.

212 Most Disney characters wear gloves in animations to simplify the drawings .

213 Movie trailers originally played after the movie.

214 'Happy Birthday' was the first song ever played on Mars. The Mars Rover Curiosity played the song to itself on its first anniversary of being on the planet.

215 Metallica is the only band that has performed on all seven continents.

216 The River Nile is the world's longest river, around 4,258 miles in length flowing through 11 countries.

217 Monaco's orchestra was once bigger than its army.

218 For the first 400 years after its invention, tennis was played using just bare hands.

219 Baseball games last for around three hours, but the average playtime is only around 18 minutes per game.

220 The first known sport was wrestling, originating in Greece in 776 BC.

221 Between 1500 and 2000 languages are spoken across the continent of Africa.

222 The most widely spoken language on the continent of Africa is Arabic. .

223 In Victorian times in the UK, clean water was rare, so instead people typically drank beer for hydration.

224 In ancient Greece, single eyebrows were a sign of beauty and intelligence.

225 A jellyfish has no ears, eyes, nose, brain or heart.

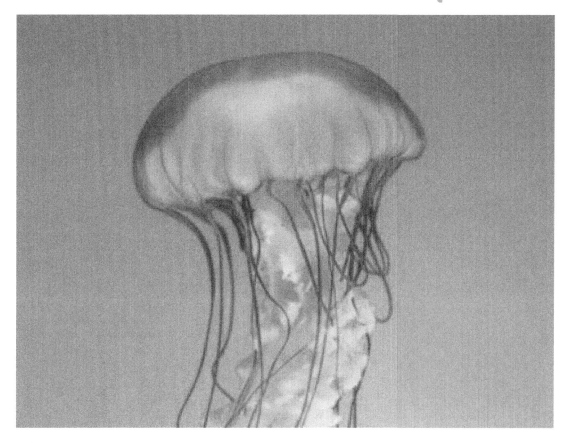

226 Only 20% of males born in the Soviet Union in the year 1923 survived World War 2.

227 Ants hate baby powder.

228 Adolf Hitler and J.R.R. Tolkien fought on opposing sides in the Battle of the Somme in World War 1.

229 There are more people in California than there are in Canada.

230 Maine is the closest point in the US to Africa.

231 Coca-Cola cannot be bought or sold in North Korea.

232 Bananas are technically radioactive. The reason why it is safe for humans to eat them is because we are more radioactive than they are.

233 The longest living animal on record is an ocean quahog clam, which is thought to have lived for 507 years.

234 A game of golf was once played on the moon.

235 Each year, the moon moves a few inches further away from Earth, meaning that it will eventually drift away.

236 The world's longest commercial flight is from New Jersey to Singapore, which takes 19 hours and travels over 9,500 miles.

237 The rate at which the continents drift around the earth is roughly the same rate at which your fingernails grow.

238 There is approximately one star for every planet in the universe. .

239 Just like we do, koalas have unique fingerprints.

240 The Hawaiian pizza was technically not invented in Hawaii, but in Canada. The name of the pizza comes from the brand of pineapple used. .

241 Iceland grows by around 5cm every year due to the movement of tectonic plates.

242 Russia has a larger surface area than Pluto, at just under a million square kilometers.

243 The group name for lemurs is a 'conspiracy'.

244 Despite Canada being north of the USA, most Canadians live south of Seattle.

245 There are more saunas in Finland than there are cars. .

There is a park ranger living in the US who has been struck by lightning seven times. . 246

247 There are over 70 varieties of mushrooms that can glow in the dark.

Believed to be rich in iron, doctors used to prescribe the beer Guinness to patients after they'd had an operation. 248

249 Elephants can die of a broken heart if their mate dies.

In a survey, it was found that 7% of American adults think chocolate milk comes from brown cows. 250

251 There is an island in Japan in which the entire population is made up of rabbits.

252 Cruise liners are legally required to have a morgue on board.

253 There is a village located in the south of Norway that is called Hell, and, ironically, it really does freeze over in the wintertime.

254 Dolly Parton once entered a Dolly Parton lookalike competition and lost.

255 Neutron stars are so dense that a tablespoon of one weighs the same as Mount Everest.

256 In Switzerland, it is illegal to own just one guinea pig.

257 Norway is simultaneously north, south, east and west of Finland.

258 The US zip code was only introduced in 1963.

259 In Iceland, some hotels have special phones that will wake you up when there are northern lights in the sky.

260 In Canada, there are only four people per square kilometer.

261 YouTube was originally launched as a video dating website. The original slogan was "Tune in, hook up."

262 Bananas are curved because they grow towards the sun.

263 The US state of Kentucky has more caves than anywhere else in the world.

264 Crows can hold grudges due to their ability to remember human faces.

265 Before becoming a famous novelist, Dan Brown, author of The da Vinci Code, had a career as a pop singer. One of his albums was called Angels and Demons.

266 North Korea and Norway are only separated by one country.

267 Most lipsticks contain fish scales.

268 Mushrooms are technically more closely related to humans than plants.

269 Raw oysters are still alive when you eat them.

270 Dinosaurs were extinct before India connected with Asia.

271 Istanbul is in both European and Asian continents.

272 The French Scrabble Word champion didn't speak French, he just memorized the entire French Scrabble dictionary which contained 386,000 words.

273 Beavers have transparent eyelids, so they can see through them as they swim under water.

274 In Ireland, palm trees grow at 53 degrees north.

275 A flame is round and blue when in zero gravity.

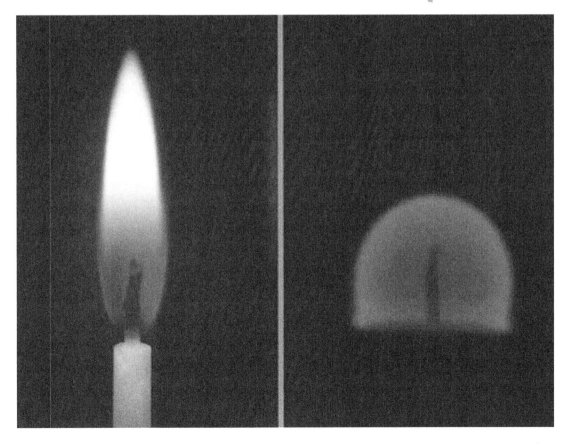

The most radioactive places at Chernobyl are not the reactor areas, but the hospital room where the clothing and equipment was left after the explosion. **276**

277 Americans eat around 20 billion hot dogs annually, which on average is around 70 hot dogs per person.

The oldest known animal alive is a tortoise born in 1832, making him 189 years old. **278**

279 Great Britain is the only country to have won a gold medal at every summer Olympic Games.

Sudan is home to more ancient pyramids than Egypt. **280**

281 Human bodies contain small traces of gold.

The acid found in a human stomach is strong enough to dissolve metal. **282**

283 The national animal of Scotland is a unicorn.

At birth, a baby octopus is around the size of a flea. **284**

285 Bluetooth technology was named after a 10th century king, Harald Bluetooth, who united Denmark and Norway.

286 In the US, squirrels are responsible for between 10 and 20% of power outages.

287 Prior to the 17th century, most carrots were purple.

288 Beethoven and George Washington were alive at the same time.

289 By 2050, the total weight of plastic in the ocean is predicted to outweigh fish.

290 Canadians eat more mac 'n' cheese than any other nation in the world.

291 90% of Earth's population lives in the Northern Hemisphere.

292 The Dead Sea is sinking at around 1 meter per year.

293 Norway is predicted to soon be completely cash-free. Currently less than 5% of transactions made in Norway are paid in cash.

294 In Copenhagen, there are more bicycles than people, and five times more bicycles than cars.

295 The Cookie Monster's real name is Sid.

296 There are over 7,000 Caribbean islands, but only around 100 are inhabited.

297 Africa is the only continent that covers four hemispheres.

298 There are more chickens in England than there are people.

299 While he studied at the University of Cambridge, Lord Byron kept a pet bear in his bedroom.

300 It is believed that there are sharks alive in the ocean today that were born in the 1700s.

DID YOU KNOW?

I LOVE YOU

EARTHWORMS HAVE FIVE HEARTS.

301 A day on Venus lasts for 5,832 hours, and on Jupiter a day is only 10 hours.

302 Nutmeg can be a hallucinogenic if consumed in large enough doses.

303 In 1849, the US presidency was technically held for just 24 hours by David Rice Atchison.

304 Actor Toni Collette faked her appendicitis so well as a teen that the doctors really removed her appendix.

305 Over the course of a lifetime you will spend around 79 days brushing your teeth.

306 Honeybees can get drunk on fermented tree sap; it makes flying difficult and can even cause them to get lost.

307 The common cold originated from camels.

308 Men are more likely to be left-handed than women.

309 A Lego brick can withstand a weight of 950 pounds.

310 One quarter of the hazelnuts produced worldwide are used to make Nutella.

311 The word 'nerd' was created by Dr Seuss.

312 The University of Oxford in England is older than the Aztec Empire.

313 Sharks have been around for about 400 million years longer than whales.

314 The town of Idyllwild in Southern California has elected a dog as its mayor.

315 The kiwi is the only bird that has nostrils at the end of its beak.

316 Every US state shares a letter with the word 'mackerel' apart from Ohio.

317 'Dreamt' is the only word in the English language that ends in 'mt'.

318 Humans and giraffes share the same number of bones in the neck .

319 The first ever text message was sent in 1992 and said 'Merry Christmas'.

320 There is not a letter 'A' in any number between 1 and 999.

321 A shrimp's heart is in its head.

322 Wearing headphones for just a single hour can increase the amount of bacteria in your ear by around 700 times.

323 Just like human fingerprints, everyone's tongue print is completely unique.

324 Sharks are the only sea creature who are known to be able to blink with both eyes at once.

325 The longest one-syllable words in the English language are 10 letters long: scraunched and strengthen.

326 There is a house sized shoe box in Amsterdam that is an Adidas store.

327 Maine is the only US state name that only has one syllable.

328 Cats have 32 muscles in each ear.

329 Tigers do not just have striped fur; they have striped skin as well.

330 Antarctica is the only continent that does not have any reptiles or snakes.

331 Snails can sleep for up to three years at a time.

332 When the pyramids were built, they were shiny and had a glass-like effect. People were appointed for the roles of polishing the stone until it shone.

333 All the termites in the world outweigh humans by a ratio of 10 to one.

334 Sea lions are the only known animal which can clap to the beat of music.

335 A typical sneeze is faster than 100 mph.

There is a name for the phobia of being watched by a duck: anatidaephobia. **336**

337 If placed in water, cans of diet soda will float but cans of regular soda will sink.

You can hear the heartbeat of a blue whale from more than two miles away. **338**

339 In one mouthful, blue whales eat around half a million calories .

The famous code that we see in The Matrix was inspired by Japanese sushi recipes. **340**

341 The Hawaiian alphabet has only 12 letters.

For three years following World War 2, the Oscar awards were made of plaster and painted. **342**

343 Sign language is recognized as an official language by 41 different countries.

Japan has more earthquakes than any country in the world. **344**

345 Four times as many people speak English as their second language than those who speak it as their native language.

The official sport of the state of Maryland is jousting.

346

347

McDonald's once paid Justin Timberlake $6 million dollars to sing their jingle.

Mosquitoes have approximately 47 teeth.

348

349

Not all twins are born on the same day. The longest period between two twins being born was 87 days.

Butterflies use their feet to taste things.

350

351 When we used the Roman calendar, February was the last month of the year which is why it has the least number of days.

352 If kept in a dark room for long enough, goldfish will turn entirely white.

353 The largest artery in the human body is the aorta, and it is nearly a foot long.

354 In the USA, the average person owns seven pairs of blue jeans.

355 The platypus does not have a stomach.

356 The brain has more fat than any other organ in the body.

357 Apes laugh when they are tickled.

358 The teddy bear is named after President Theodore Roosevelt.

359 Mice can fit through extremely small gaps – even the hole of a ballpoint pen.

360 The inspiration for the shape of Pac-Man was a pizza with one slice removed from it.

361 As humans, we share 50% of our genes with bananas.

362 Mosquitoes kill more people than any other creature on earth.

363 Every second, it is estimated that four people are born while two will die.

364 Crabs have taste buds on their feet.

365 The first digital computer was programed by a team of six women.

366 Baby elephants suck their trunks for comfort, just like humans do with their thumbs.

367 Birds would not be able to survive in space as they rely on gravity to be able to swallow.

368 When we fly in an airplane, we lose around 30% of our sense of taste.

369 A blue whale's heart is around the size of a golf cart, weighing 630 times the weight of a human heart.

370 On Jupiter and Saturn, it rains diamonds.

371 A glass ball can bounce higher than a rubber ball of the same size.

372 Ants have an even stronger sense of smell than dogs.

373 The people alive today represent only around 7% of those who have ever been alive.

374 Thomas Jefferson kept pet grizzly bears.

375 The most popular name throughout the entire world is Muhammad.

376 Australia has a lake that is bright pink, caused by an unusual mixture of natural salt and algae in the water.

377 Beavers used to be the size of bears.

378 Penguins can jump as high as 9ft into the air.

379 The sunsets on Mars are blue rather than orange or red.

380 Cotton candy was invented by a dentist.

381 Los Angeles has more cars than people.

382 Armadillos can become buoyant when they swim by swallowing air.

383 The entire city of Paris has only one stop sign.

384 There is a heavy metal band whose lead singer is a parrot.

385 Cameron Diaz and Snoop Dogg went to school together.

Two-thirds of the world's population has never seen real snow. 386

387 You technically do not have to be a lawyer to be a Supreme Court Justice.

The human eye typically makes around 50 tiny movements every second. 388

389 The average human scalp has over 100,000 hair follicles.

At birth, a baby panda is smaller than a mouse. 390

391 Dentistry is one of the oldest known profession, with records dating back to 7000 BC.

Football, rugby, golf, boxing and cricket were all invented in the UK. 392

393 There is a village in the Netherlands with no streets, only canals.

John Quincy Adams was gifted a pet alligator by a French general, which he kept in a bathtub in the White House. 394

395 Cows have been proven to produce more milk when they are listening to music.

DID YOU KNOW?

SCIENTIFIC STUDIES DISCOVERED THAT MICROWAVING FOOD DOES NOT DIMINISH NUTRIENTS.

Four out of 10 of the largest statues in the world are of Buddha. **396**

397 Around half of all US adults currently have a Netflix subscription.

The first planet that was predicted before it was physically seen was Neptune. **398**

399 The world record for the tallest ever stack of donuts is more than 3,000.

11 US states have land further south than the northern part of Mexico. **400**

401 A cat's tail contains nearly 10% of all the bones in its body.

402 Abraham Lincoln was inducted into the National Wrestling Hall of Fame, having only ever lost once in 300 matches.

403 There is a vending machine in Singapore that dispenses Coke when you hug it.

404 The longest place name on the planet is 85 letters long.

405 It takes the average person just seven minutes to fall asleep.

406 From a botanical perspective, a banana is technically an herb rather than a fruit.

407 It is not possible to sneeze in your sleep.

408 Avocadoes will not ripen when still on the tree, only after they have been picked.

409 Ducklings will 'imprint' with whoever they meet within the first few minutes of birth. If that is a human, it will consider them its parent forever.

410 43 countries still have a royal family.

411 The tongue of a blue whale is heavier than an elephant, weighing more than 7,000kg.

412 The ocean contains more than 200,000 different kinds of viruses.

413 Abraham Lincoln was a licensed bartender.

414 Your sense of smell will begin to improve within only two days of quitting smoking.

415 LSD or acid was legal in California up until 1966.

416 President John Tyler, born in 1790, has a grandson who is still alive today.

417 Cheetahs do not roar; they make a sound that is very like that of a house cat.

418 Hawaii is the only US state that has just one school district.

419 The first ever telephone book was released in 1878 and contained 50 names.

420 Benjamin Franklin is in the International Swimming Hall of Fame.

421 There are more Lego figures on Earth than there are people.

422 There is a ski-through McDonald's in Sweden.

423 About 40 million years ago, there is evidence to suggest that penguins were 6ft tall.

424 Hippo sweat is red in color which also acts as a natural sunscreen.

425 The thigh bone (femur) is both the longest and strongest bone in the human body.

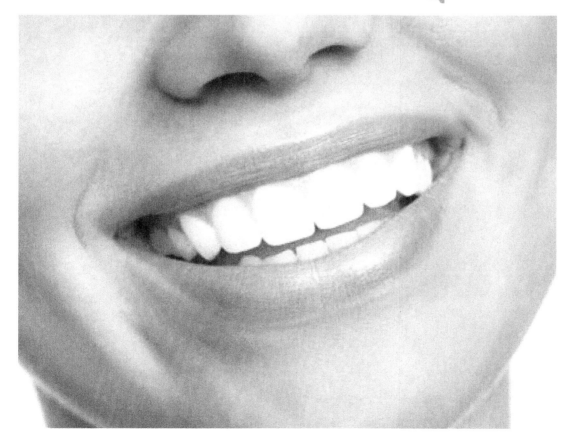

426 If put back into place, teeth can reattach to their roots.

427 Only two national flags in the world contain purple: Dominica and Nicaragua.

428 The shortest word for a study of something is 'oology', the study of bird eggs.

429 The term 'astronaut' comes from the Greek words that mean 'star' and 'sailor'.

430 Most of the polar bears in the world live in Canada rather than the Artic.

431 The highest wave to ever be surfed was as tall as a 10-story building.

432 The best-selling book of all time is the Bible with more than 5 billion copies sold.

433 Iceland has no mosquitoes.

434 Sloths can live up to 30 years and spend 15-18 hours a day sleeping.

435 The Australian Alps get more snow than the Swiss Alps.

436 We miss approximately 10% of everything we see due to blinking.

437 Brass doorknobs automatically disinfect themselves within eight hours.

438 George Harrison could play 26 instruments.

439 November 19th is international 'have a bad day' day.

440 The tallest ever recorded human was 8'11.

441 Bubble wrap was first created as wallpaper.

442 There are no rivers in Saudi Arabia.

443 The Lockheed SR-71 Blackbird has held the record of the fastest manned jet aircraft since 1976, flying at 2,193 miles per hour.

444 Cashews grow on a cashew apple which is attached to a tree.

445 A full jumbo-jet tank has enough fuel for a car to drive around the entire world four times.

446 Potatoes contain nearly every nutrient that humans need to survive.

447 1,000 selfies are posted to Instagram every 10 seconds, equating to 93 million selfies every day.

448 Walt Disney has won more Oscars than anyone else in history, a total of 22.

449 It is impossible to predict whether there is going to be turbulence on a plane.

450 The average iPhone costs just $200 to make.

451 Chanel and Louis Vuitton were the first ever designer logo's .

452 Tutankhamun's tomb remained completely sealed for 3245 years until 1922.

453 The stickers found on fruit are FDA-approved, making them completely edible.

454 You can buy eel flavored ice cream in Japan.

455 Mantis shrimps can punch with the force of a bullet.

A group of flamingos is called a 'flamboyance'. 456

457 In Arizona, it is against the law to have a sleeping donkey in your bathtub after 7pm.

The longest ever tennis match lasted over 12 hours. 458

459 In Indonesia, there is a word for tapping someone on the wrong shoulder to fool them: 'menfolk'.

Earth is the only planet that is not named after a god. 460

461 The company Nintendo is more than 100 years old and began as a card game business.

The small intestine is longer than the large intestine. 462

463 Machu Picchu is an earthquake-proof city due to the way the bricks were constructed.

The opah, or sunfish, was the first warm-blooded fish discovered in the world. 364

465 A chameleon's tongue is double the length of its body.

466 The largest mouth of any animal is that of a hippo.

467 There are books within Harvard University that are bound in human skin.

468 In Florida, it is illegal to pass wind in public after 6pm on a Thursday.

469 It takes 12 bees a lifetime of work to make one teaspoon of honey.

470 Otters have the thickest fur in the animal kingdom .

471 France is the most popular tourist destination in the world. In 2017, it had more than 86 million visitors.

472 It's a myth that humans use less than 10% of their brain.

473 Jupiter is bigger than all other planets in the solar system combined.

474 On a clear day, you can see Alaska from Russia and vice versa.

475 Humans have been eating sugar for around 10,000 years.

When in zero-gravity conditions, flames appear round and blue rather than yellow. 476

477 Coca-Cola sells 1.9 billion drinks worldwide every day.

Ostriches' eyes are bigger than their brains. 478

479 Earth is hit by lightning 100 times every second.

In Greece, it is against the law for women to wear high heels or tall hats inside the Olympic Stadium. 480

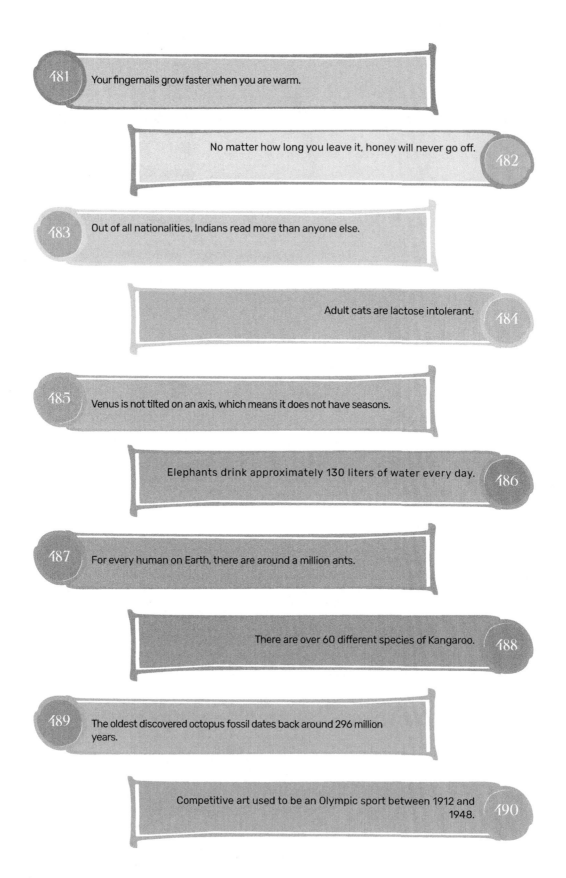

481 Your fingernails grow faster when you are warm.

482 No matter how long you leave it, honey will never go off.

483 Out of all nationalities, Indians read more than anyone else.

484 Adult cats are lactose intolerant.

485 Venus is not tilted on an axis, which means it does not have seasons.

486 Elephants drink approximately 130 liters of water every day.

487 For every human on Earth, there are around a million ants.

488 There are over 60 different species of Kangaroo.

489 The oldest discovered octopus fossil dates back around 296 million years.

490 Competitive art used to be an Olympic sport between 1912 and 1948.

491 12 US States have a place called Long Beach.

492 Pluto is smaller in diameter than the United States.

493 The African driver ant can produce up to 4 million eggs per month.

494 Humans can only survive without oxygen for three minutes.

495 In Samoa, it is illegal to forget your wife's birthday.

496 Male seahorses carry offspring and give birth, not the females.

497 Due to the Earth's rotation, you can throw an object further if you throw it west.

498 It is illegal for citizens to make offensive gestures at passing cars in Zimbabwe.

499 The Mona Lisa has no eyebrows.

500 Only around 20% of Earth's deserts are sandy.

501 Every single continent begins and ends with the same letter.

502 The most expensive coffee in the world can cost more than $600 for a single pound.

503 If we did not have saliva, we would no longer be able to taste food.

504 Your right hand has never touched your right elbow.

505 The hottest chili pepper in the world has the power to kill a human.

506 Pigs cannot look up at the sky, in fact it is physically impossible.

507 The longest word in the English language without vowels is 'rhythms'.

508 There is a town in Chile called Calama where it almost never rains.

509 Humans and tree shrews are the only animal that enjoys spicy foods.

510 The saying 'sweating like a pig' is peculiar considering pigs cannot sweat.

511 Your nose is always visible to you, but your mind ignores it most of the time.

512 More Monopoly money is printed each year than real money.

513 Switzerland and Vatican City are the only nations with a square flag.

514 The Hogwarts Express is a real train on which you can travel in Scotland.

515 Elephants are known to suffer from PTSD.

516 Honey from the Himalayan honeybee is hallucinogenic.

517 Bumblebees can fly higher than Mount Everest.

518 Pigeons produce milk to feed their young.

519 The longest that anyone ever had the hiccups was 68 years.

520 Vincent Van Gogh only sold one painting in his lifetime.

521 The code name for the Queen of England dying is 'Operation London Bridge'.

522 Dogs can be trained to smell cancer, which is being developed into life-saving technology.

523 Lego produces more tires per year than any other manufacturer.

524 The Empire State Building has its own ZIP code.

525 It would take around 18 months to walk the length of the Great Wall of China.

526 350 million years ago, there are thought to be 20ft high mushrooms.

527 You can pay to go on expeditions with National Geographic to exotic places like Antarctica.

528 One in every 200 men alive today in central Asia is descendent of Genghis Khan .

529 The word 'set' has more definitions than any other word in the English language.

530 The inventor of the font Comic Sans only used it once, and claims he does not like it.

531 The grooves in the road on Route 66 play 'America the Beautiful' if driven over at 45mph.

532 Snow on Venus is made from metal.

533 To this day, scientists do not know how dinosaurs mated.

534 India has a bill of rights dedicated to just cows.

535 Before designing the Barbie Doll, Jack Ryan had designed military grade missiles.

The first-ever identical twin birds were emus. **536**

537 Every single Pixar movie contains a reference for the following Pixar movie .

Russia has more forest than any other country. **538**

539 Four different states are visible from the top of Chicago's Willis Tower.

Violin and cello bows are made from horse hair. **540**

541 There are five countries in the world that do not have an airport.

Ants stretch when they wake up, just like humans. **542**

543 Niagara Falls never freezes.

Big Ben in London has started leaning to one side – the lean can now be seen by the naked eye. **544**

545 Umpires of Major League Baseball must contractually wear black underwear in case their pants split.

546 The US army once had more ships than the US navy .

547 Craving ice is a known symptom of iron deficiency.

548 Oxygen has a pale blue color in both solid and liquid form.

549 Only 3% of water on Earth is pure water, the rest contains salt.

550 The fat content of a carrot is zero.

551 French fries come from Belgium, not France.

552 Coffee beans are actually fruit pits not beans.

553 It only takes brain cells six minutes to react to alcohol.

554 Frozen water takes up about 9% more volume than liquid water.

555 Ketchup leaves the bottle at a rate of 25 miles per year.

The Bible is the most stolen book in the world. 556

557 Billboards are banned in Vermont.

Bats are the only mammals that can fly. 558

559 An average elephant can hold 4 liters of water in its trunk.

The fear of cheese is called 'turophobia'. 560

561 Some Armadillo shells are bullet proof.

There was one known death in WW2 that was carried out using a longbow. 562

563 Tomatoes have more genes than humans.

There is a restaurant in the Canary Islands where food is served cooked using geothermal heat from a volcano. 564

565 It is possible for turtles to drown.

566 Without tails, kangaroos would not be able to hop.

567 A lead pencil can be used to write a line that is 56km long.

568 The first computer mouse in 1964 was made of wood.

569 Geckos eat their skin when they shed it to prevent predators from being able to find them.

570 Alpacas can die from loneliness, so they need to live in pairs or more.

571 There is an Asian animal called a 'raccoon dog'. It looks like a raccoon but it is actually a dog.

Around 100 people die each year from choking on ballpoint pens. 572

573 A jiffy is a real measure of time – around 10 milliseconds.

Glass can be recycled endlessly without losing quality or purity. 574

575 Tasmania has the cleanest air in the world, besides Antarctica .

An elephant's trunk contains 150,000 muscles. 576

577 Major league baseballs are never used for more than seven pitches.

Phobia of the belly button is called 'omphalophobia'. 578

579 There were 8 deaths on the Titanic before the ship even set sail.

Rainbows can only occur when the sun is 40 degrees or less above the horizon. 580

581 Silk is the strongest known natural material, which is five times stronger than steel.

582 The longest ever mustache recorded was 14 feet long.

583 It is possible to fracture a rib from sneezing.

584 Skunks are immune to snake venom.

585 Dolphins have two stomachs, one for storing food and one for digestion.

586 The surface water in the Atlantic Ocean is saltier than that of the Pacific Ocean.

587 The only class that Elvis Presley failed in school was music class.

588 Giraffes do not have vocal cords.

589 One in four Americans have appeared on TV.

590 Three dogs survived the Titanic sinking.

591 During the Christmas period, nearly 28 sets of Lego are sold every second.

592 Lettuce is a member of the sunflower family.

593 It is illegal in Atlanta, Georgia to tie a giraffe to a telephone pole or street lamp.

594 Moths do not have stomachs.

595 The original name for Google was 'Backrub'.

596 In the 1900s, teams competed in the Olympics at tug of war.

597 Mr. Potato Head was the first toy ever advertised on TV.

598 Two is the only even prime number.

599 The world's largest scoop of ice cream weighed more than 3,000lbs.

600 A frog's tongue is about a third of the length of its whole body.

601 `Coral is closer to an animal than it is to a plant.

602 Some blizzards are made up of sand rather than snow.

603 Cows' moos have regional accents.

604 We still sweat when we are swimming, but we just don't notice.

605 A 10-year-old mattress weighs double its original weight.

606 The human bone is stronger than steel, but it breaks more easily because it is brittle.

607 Chocolate ice cream has been shown to reduce physical pain.

608 The Bible has been translated into more than 3,000 languages.

609 The world's oldest chewing gum is 5,000 years old.

610 There is a spa in Japan where you can swim in wine.

611 Cucumber can kill bacteria and therefore can get rid of bad breath.

612 If two pieces of the same metal touch in space, they will permanently bond together.

613 There is a house in Massachusetts that is made entirely out of newspaper.

614 There has never been more carbon dioxide in the atmosphere than there is right now.

615 Ontario, Canada has more than 250,000 lakes.

616 Our little fingers contribute to 50% of our hand strength.

617 Only female mosquitoes bite humans.

618 The blue whale produces around 1200 liters of urine per day.

619 Lizards can self-amputate if they need to, and the limb will grow back.

620 There is a sinkhole in Belize that is 410 feet deep.

621 The smallest bat in the world weighs less than a dime.

622 You can make honey from dandelions.

623 It is illegal to carry pliers in Texas.

624 In Berlin, aggressive sitting is a recognized sport.

625 None of the members of The Beatles could read music.

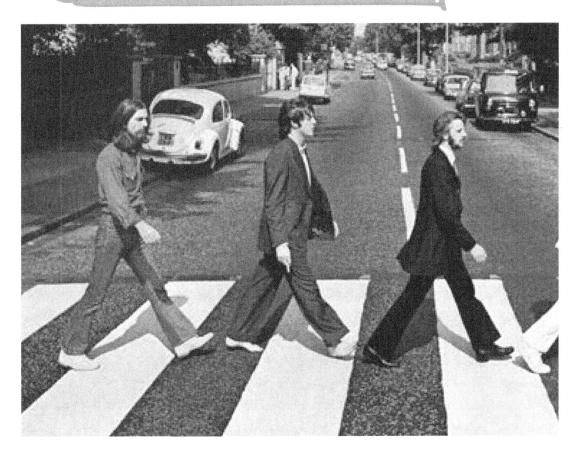

631 Mosquitoes cannot penetrate silk.

632 Mary Queen of Scots became Queen at only six days old.

633 The Walt Disney World Resort is roughly the same size as San Francisco.

634 Oak trees only begin producing acorns when they reach around 50 years of age.

635 Humans did not come from monkeys, but we do share a common ancestor.

626 Any misdemeanor towards a camel is illegal in Arizona.

627 Joe Biden became the oldest ever US president.

628 85% of Valentine's Day cards are bought by women.

629 In Finland, you can throw mobile phones for sport.

630 The thinnest skin on the body is on the eyelids.

636 There are more than 4.48 billion active social media users worldwide.

637 There are more beetles in the world than any other animal.

638 Lions have unique whisker patterns, much like a human fingerprint.

639 Eyebrow hairs will shed and entirely renew around every two months.

640 In 2001, red rain fell on western India, dying everyone's clothes pink.

641 Bamboo grows so fast that it is measured in miles per hour.

642 Humpback whales will let dolphins ride on their back.

643 The largest ever turtle weighed more than a ton.

644 The sun is the most perfect sphere that can be observed in nature.

645 Male honeybees only mate on one occasion, they die soon afterwards.

646 Leeches have a brain in all 32 parts of their bodies.

647 The United States does not have an official language.

648 Texas has the most colleges of all the US states.

649 The most common time to wake in the night is 3:44am.

650 In Ancient Greece, pigeons delivered the results of the Olympic Games.

651 The USA has the most dogs out of any country.

652 Florida is the only state on the east coast that falls partially in the Central Time Zone.

653 It's illegal to sell photos of the Eiffel Tower that have been taken at night.

654 Of the 25 highest peaks in the world, 10 are in the Himalayas.

655 All ATMs at the Vatican are in Latin.

656 Walt Disney kept live animals on the set of some of his films to inspire the animation team.

657 French poodles are actually German.

658 The most spoken word worldwide is 'OK'.

659 Its estimated that 80% of lawyers in the world are in the United States.

660 Russia is the third closest neighbor to the United States.

661 Color television was invented in Mexico in 1946.

662 The word 'makeup' was coined by cosmetic entrepreneur Max Factor.

663 Most birds do not have a sense of smell.

664 To officially form a coven, there must be a total of 13 witches.

665 Solitaire is the most widely played card game in the world.

666 Tiffany's supplied the Union army with swords during the American Civil War.

667 Polar bears can swim for 60 miles without stopping.

668 A cricket's ears are on its front legs.

669 The name for the unfilled space between the bottle top and the liquid is known as the 'ullage'.

670 The state of Virginia goes further west than the state of West Virginia.

671 There are no landlocked countries in North America.

672 Bagpipes were invented in the Middle East.

673 The French drink more than 26 million liters of wine each year.

674 Sound travels four times faster in water than in air.

675 Abraham Lincoln was the first ever Republican president.

676 We have an average of four to six dreams per night.

677 Lichtenstein is the biggest exporter of false teeth in the world.

678 San Francisco is 80% water and 20% land.

679 Lemons float in water and limes sink.

680 Cats cannot taste sweet things.

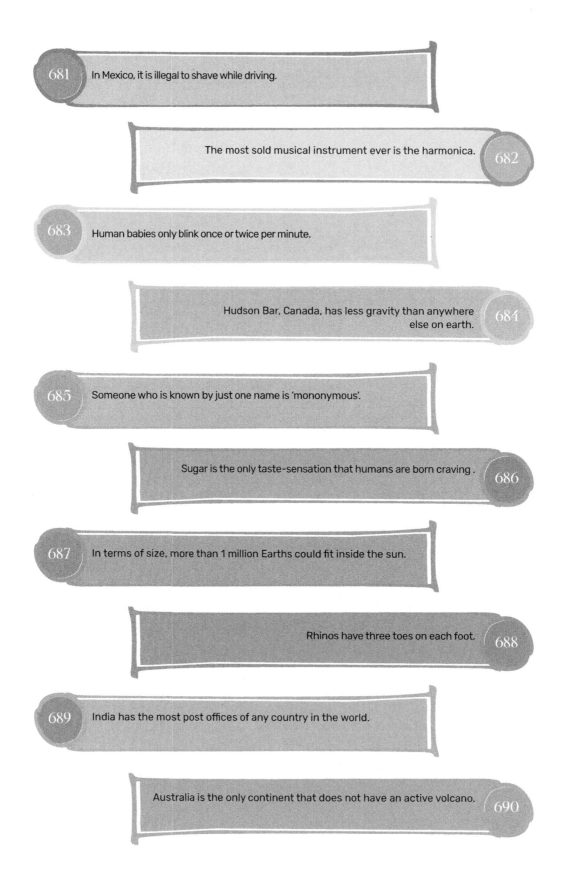

681 In Mexico, it is illegal to shave while driving.

682 The most sold musical instrument ever is the harmonica.

683 Human babies only blink once or twice per minute.

684 Hudson Bar, Canada, has less gravity than anywhere else on earth.

685 Someone who is known by just one name is 'mononymous'.

686 Sugar is the only taste-sensation that humans are born craving.

687 In terms of size, more than 1 million Earths could fit inside the sun.

688 Rhinos have three toes on each foot.

689 India has the most post offices of any country in the world.

690 Australia is the only continent that does not have an active volcano.

691 Teeth are the only part of the body that cannot repair themselves.

692 Pablo Picasso has had his work stolen more than any other artist.

693 The Sargasso Sea is the only sea that does not have a coastline.

694 New York City is further south than Rome, Italy.

695 On average, we spend six years of our lives dreaming.

696 Shark skin used to be used as commercial sandpaper.

697 Antarctica is the continent with the most wind.

698 Mayans and Aztecs used to use cocoa beans as currency.

699 The first-ever products in aerosol cans were insecticides.

700 The most widely eaten meat is pork, with poultry and beef in second place.

701 The Tour de France has been running for more than 100 years.

702 Yawning cools down your brain.

703 Broccoli contains more protein than steak.

704 Sharks do not technically sleep, their brains are always at least partially awake.

705 The air in crisp bags is nitrogen, which is used to keep the contents fresh.

706 Pocahontas was the first Disney animated film based on a real person.

707 Joseph Priestley invented carbonated water before later discovering oxygen.

708 Giraffes have the longest tails of any animals; they can be up to 8ft long.

709 France is the biggest country in the EU, but is still smaller than Texas.

710 Coffee grounds are highly effective as ant repellent.

711 Hot dogs are not American, they are thought to have originated from Austria.

712 The longest TV advertisement in history is 14 hours long.

713 The human body contains around 45 miles of nerves.

714 Australia, New Zealand and South Korea all fought in the Vietnam War.

715 The whip was the first man-made invention to break the sound barrier.

716 The comma is the most used punctuation mark.

717 The largest immigrant group in Mexico is US citizens.

718 Nearly all kangaroos are left-handed.

719 It is possible to get hiccups due to a fast change in temperature.

720 On average, we spend three months of our lives on the toilet.

721 The owner of the Segway Company died while riding a Segway.

722 Tomatoes contain a small amount of nicotine.

723 Killer whales are actually dolphins.

724 The average Antarctica ice sheet is one mile thick.

725 The Statue of Liberty originally also served as a lighthouse, guiding boats safely to land.

726 The state of California is the world's 5th biggest food supplier.

727 Dwight D. Eisenhower was the first US president to govern all 50 states.

728 The tongue heals faster than any other part of the human body.

729 The potter's wheel predates democracy by around 5,000 years.

730 In poker, more than 300 million 7-card hand combinations exist.

731 On Mount Rushmore, the nose of George Washington is 21 feet long.

732 At Starbucks, there are approximately 87,000 drink combinations that can be requested.

733 Florence Nightingale used to carry an owl in her pocket.

734 The concept of speed dating was invented by a Rabbi.

735 In France, the most toilet paper sold is pink rather than white.

736 The average American consumes almost 10lbs of cereal each year.

737 Harry S. Truman's middle name was S. It did not stand for anything.

738 Israeli postage stamps use kosher certified glue.

739 The folding bed was invented in ancient Greece.

740 Eminem got the idea for his Slim Shady character while on the toilet.

741 Earth is the only planet in the solar system where fire can burn.

742 The word 'hundred' comes from the Norse language and originally means 120.

743 It is estimated that a species becomes extinct every 20 minutes.

744 Its estimated that the Black Death killed around half the population of London.

745 In Panama, you can watch the sun rising on the Pacific Ocean and setting on the Atlantic Ocean.

746 A full-moon is 6 times brighter than a half-moon.

747 Strawberries are grown in every state in the USA and every province in Canada.

748 The King of Hearts is the only king in a deck of cards that does not have a moustache.

749 An albatross can take short naps while flying.

750 Wind does not make a sound until it blows against an object.

751 The global population is growing by around 83 million people each year.

752 The fewest number of turns it takes to solve a Rubik's cube is 17.

753 There are more Siberian tigers in zoos than in the wild.

754 More than 50% of people yawn when they read the word 'yawn'.

755 It is impossible to tickle yourself.

756 At a latitude of 60 degrees south, you can sail around the entire world without seeing land.

757 Camels can drink 25 gallons of water in under three minutes.

758 Koalas do not typically drink any water at all, and will only do so in cases of extreme heat.

759 The big toe has two bones while the other toes all have three.

760 Flying fish can leap out of water at a speed of 20mph and can fly for more than 500ft.

761 Potatoes have more chromosomes than human beings.

762 There are no recorded cases of killer whales having ever killed a human in the wild.

763 Oswald the Lucky Rabbit was the first Disney character, not Mickey Mouse.

764 Concrete is the most used man-made material on earth.

765 Pelicans can hold more food in their beaks than in their stomachs.

766 Unlike domesticated cats, Siberian tigers love swimming.

767 There is zero fat in carrots.

768 Oysters can change gender multiple times in their lifetime.

769 There are more ghost towns in Oregon than in any other US state.

770 The Liberty Bell strikes in the note E-flat.

771 Africa holds around 30% of the world's mineral resources.

772 Planet Earth is located inside the sun's atmosphere.

773 Caterpillars have more muscles than humans.

774 Toe wrestling is a competitive sport.

775 A hippo can remain completely underwater for as long as five minutes.

776 Lara Croft was originally going to be called Laura Cruz.

777 Leopards can stay in the same position for up to 8 hours.

778 Nicolas Cage suggested Jonny Depp get involved in acting.

779 On February 18, 1930, Elm Farm Ollie became the first cow to fly in an airplane.

780 Only 2% of the earth's population has green eyes.

781 Peregrine falcons are used by airports in the United States to help keep birds off the runway.

782 Hans Asperger identified autism in 1944.

783 Hypnophobia is the fear of falling asleep.

784 It has been scientifically proven that alcohol increases creativity.

785 It is a rule of the New York Mafia families that they are not allowed to grow facial hair.

786 It is possible to get cancer of the heart, but it is very rare.

787 The Pringles cartoon mascot man's name is Julius.

788 The Republic of Madagascar is the 4th-largest island in the world. .

789 Uranus is the only planet that rotates on its side.

790 Vampire bats urinate on whatever animal they are drinking from.

791 Venice, Italy, sinks about 1 to 2 mm a year and is slowly tilting to the east.

792 A palm tree isn't really a tree; it's a type of grass.

793 A toxic dose of ground nutmeg is 2 to 3 teaspoons.

794 Abu Dhabi has a beauty contest for camels.

795 Dora the Explorer's real name is Dora Márquez.

796 Drinking too much water (water intoxication) can kill you.

797 An African elephant only has four teeth.

798 Due to the shortage of metal during WWII, the Oscars trophies were made of painted plaster.

799 Everyone's tongue print is unique.

800 Men, generally speaking, are able to read smaller print than woman.

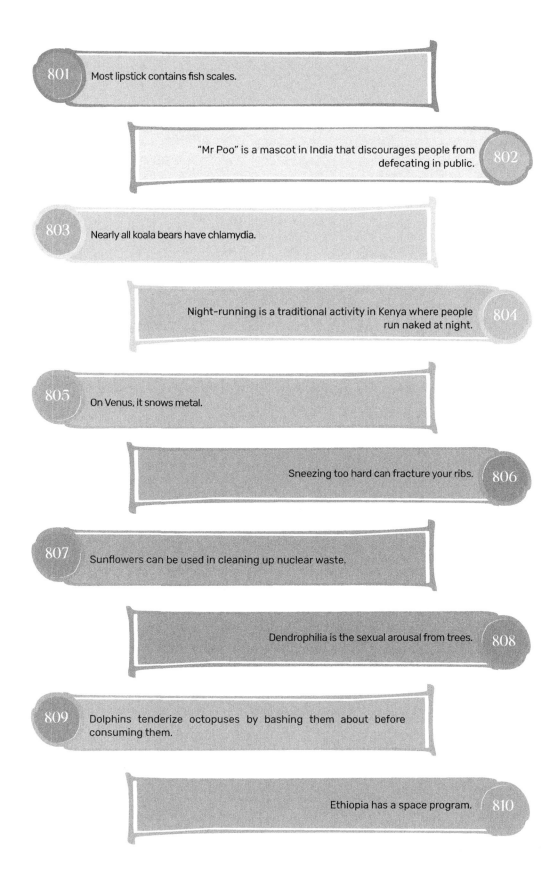

801 Most lipstick contains fish scales.

802 "Mr Poo" is a mascot in India that discourages people from defecating in public.

803 Nearly all koala bears have chlamydia.

804 Night-running is a traditional activity in Kenya where people run naked at night.

805 On Venus, it snows metal.

806 Sneezing too hard can fracture your ribs.

807 Sunflowers can be used in cleaning up nuclear waste.

808 Dendrophilia is the sexual arousal from trees.

809 Dolphins tenderize octopuses by bashing them about before consuming them.

810 Ethiopia has a space program.

811 Avocados are poisonous to birds (which means more guacamole for us).

812 Babies are born with 300 bones (compared to the 206 found in adults).

813 Beetles taste like apples.

814 Birds don't urinate.

815 People with blue eyes have a higher tolerance to alcohol.

816 Pretty much anything that melts can be made into glass.

817 Prostitutes in the Netherlands pay taxes.

818 Russia has about the same surface area as Pluto.

819 Cats rub against people and furniture to mark their territory.

820 \Charles Darwin ate a specimen of nearly every animal he discovered.

821 Clams can live for more than 400 years.

822 Deer can starve to death with a stomach full of hay.

823 A group of ravens is called an unkindness.

824 A group of starlings is called a murmuration.

825 A group of wild rabbits are called a fluffle.

Ravens have been observed pretending to hide food in one place before quietly hiding it in another to throw off other ravens. 826

827 Australia has a larger population of camels than Egypt.

Australia's dingo fence is longer than the Great Wall of China. 828

829 Brian May, guitarist of Queen, is an astrophysicist.

Hippopotamus milk is pink. 830

831 Caesar salad has nothing to do with any of the Caesars. It was first concocted in a bar in Tijuana, Mexico, in the 1920's.

Your fingernails grow faster when you are cold. 832

833 Snails take the longest naps, some lasting as long as three years.

Though closely identified as a female fashion staple today, high heels were first designed for men. 834

835 Your sense of touch fades as you age.

836 Tuskless elephants are evolving in response to poaching.

837 Male pufferfish create "crop circles" to attract mates.

838 There's a city in Turkey called Batman, located in the provinc.

839 The opossum is the only marsupial in North America.

840 Walmart employs 2.3 million people around the world.

841 New York City has the area code 212 because rotary phones were used at the time, and the number uses the shortest dialing time.

842 In January of 2013, the finance minister of Zimbabwe announced that his country had only 217 dollars left in its bank account.

843 There is a humpback whale that has been tracked by Greenpeace since 2008 called Mr. Splashy Pants.

844 You can pay to go on expeditions with National Geographic to exotic places like Antarctica.

845 There's a golf course in Brisbane, Australia with full grown bull sharks living in the water hazards.

The Pineberry is a white strawberry that tastes like a pineapple. **846**

847 An average elephant can hold and store four liters of water in its trunk.

Spain offers citizenship to the descendants of those who came to the Americas to flee the Inquisition. **848**

849 A snake cannot blink at all.

3.5 billion years ago, a mega-asteroid that was likely 30 miles across slammed into Earth in Australia. **850**

851 The horned lizard has blood-filled sinuses within the eye sockets that squirt blood in self-defense by swelling and rupturing.

852 Alaska has the longest coastline in the United States at 6,640 miles long.

853 The oldest octopus fossil was discovered in northeast Illinois U.S. It dates back approximately 296 million years.

854 Ronald Reagan and Donald Trump are the only two divorced men to ever be elected president. That includes more than two centuries worth of U.S. presidential elections.

855 If you keep a goldfish in the dark, it will become pale.

856 Research conducted at the University of Stanford concluded that a racially diverse group has the ability to solve problems more effectively than a group with only one race in it.

857 Olympic gold medals are made of silver.

858 Actual playing time in a major league baseball game is on average less than 18 minutes.

859 When you think of a past event, you remember the last time you remembered it, not the occasion itself.

860 Giving up alcohol for just one month is very healthy. It improves liver function, decreases blood pressure, and reduces the risk of liver disease and diabetes.

861 The consumption of sugary drinks is linked to 180,000 deaths per year.

862 "Cars.com" was the most expensive domain name ever sold. Astonishing fact, that it cost $872.3 million.

863 About 25% of all blood coming from the heart goes into the kidneys.

864 Without saliva, humans aren't able to taste food.

865 Approximately 1 in 2,000 babies already has a tooth when it is born.

866 Money is made in factories called mints.

867 The first paper money was made in China over 1,000 years ago.

868 A dime has 118 ridges around the edge.

869 A baby panda right after birth is smaller than a mouse.

870 The veins of a blue whale are so big a child could swim through them.

871 Frogs drink water through their skin.

872 A crocodile cannot stick its tongue out.

873 Snails take the longest-lasting naps, some last as long as 3 years.

874 Some fish cough. Really.

875 Goats have rectangular pupils in their eyes.

876 Cats have 32 muscles in each ear.

877 An ostrich's brain is smaller than its eye.

878 Tigers have not only striped fur, but also striped skin.

879 A slug has four noses.

880 Hippopotamuses can run faster than humans.

881 An apple is one of the few fruits that float on water.

882 The number four is the only number with the same number of letters used to write it.

883 You cannot inhale or exhale while you are talking.

884 It is impossible to hum while holding your nose closed.

885 Pluto is so small that the United States is bigger than it is.

886 Earth is the only planet in our solar system that is not named after some kind of god.

887 No one knows who named our planet "Earth."

888 Venus has more volcanoes on its surface than any other planet in the solar system.

889 A collection of geese is referred to as a "gaggle."

890 Women purchase 96% of the candles that are sold.

891 Domesticated cats hate the smell of citrus.

892 A tiger's skin is striped just like its fur.

893 An ostrich's eye is so big that its brain is smaller than its eye.

894 A gorilla can get sick, just like humans can.

895 Bats are the only mammals on Earth that can fly!

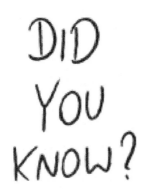

DID YOU KNOW?

CHEESE IS THE MOST STOLEN FOOD IN THE WORLD. 4% OF ALL CHEESE ENDS UP BEING STOLEN.

There are around 45,000 thunderstorms occurring around the world every day. **896**

897 For some reason, the average Canadian earns more than the average American and is therefore richer.

There are around 1,500 earthquakes in Japan happening every year. **898**

899 Diamonds actually are not as rare as you may think. They are very easy to find on Earth.

The country Brazil was named after a tree. **900**

901 The country Brazil makes up 50% of the South American continent.

There are around 120 different rivers in Jamaica. 902

903 The Great Wall of China is around 3,995 miles long.

Humans share 60% of our DNA with bananas! 904

905 The Cesky Terrier (around 350 of them exist in total, worldwide) is the rarest breed of dog in the world.

Turkey sure does love tea. They consume the most tea per person in the world. That is almost seven pounds of tea a year. 906

907 Tonic water can actually glow in the dark!

A shark can swim up to 44 miles per hour. 908

909 Apples contain 25% air, and that is why they float on water.

Bats are the only mammals in the world that can fly. 910

911 Bananas grow while pointing upwards.

912 A whale cannot swim backward.

913 The number "one googol" is basically one followed by 100 zeros.

914 The largest organ on the human body is the skin.

915 No one knows where the original copy of the Declaration of Independence is. There is a handwritten copy of the original in Washington, D.C.

916 Over half of all court cases in the U.S. are traffic-related.

917 A 2013 study found that the U.S. Congress was less popular among Americans than cockroaches and traffic jams.

918 The first professional police officer in Stewartstown, Pennsylvania was also the town lamp lighter. He was hired in 1876.

919 In California, prison inmates are used to fight forest fires.

920 The modern system of 911 emergency communications was developed in Lincoln, Nebraska.

921 Jimmy Carter was the first U.S. president to be born in a hospital.

922 Only one U.S. president's wife was born in another country: Louisa Adams, wife of John Quincy Adams.

923 Every president of the United States who had a beard was a Republican.

924 Every president of the United States has had siblings.

925 Abraham Lincoln, the 16th president of the United States, was a licensed bartender.

926 Maine is the U.S.'s largest producer of both lobsters and blueberries.

927 About 2 billion pounds of chocolate are consumed each year in the U.S.

928 Margarine was once illegal in Wisconsin.

929 The dry breakfast cereal industry was started when the Kellogg brothers accidentally figured out how to make flaked cereal.

930 There's only one steam-powered cider mill in the U.S. It's located in Mystic, Connecticut.

931 Plant City, Florida is the "Winter Strawberry Capital of the World."

932 In a few Appalachian forests, some fireflies glow blue instead of flashing yellow.

933 The Reuben sandwich was invented in Nebraska.

934 France gave the United States its famous Statue of Liberty in 1884.

935 The first country to recognize the newly independent United States in 1776 was the Republic of Ragusa, which is now part of Croatia.

936 The last signature on the Declaration of Independence was added 5 years after the United States declared its independence.

937 After World War II, Japan sent cherry trees to the state of Utah to symbolize friendship.

938 During the Civil War, hundreds of women dressed as men in order to serve in the war.

939 Badwater Basin in Death Valley, California is the lowest point in the western hemisphere. It is 282 feet below sea level.

940 The deepest lake in the U.S. is five times the height of the Statue of Liberty. It is located in the state of Oregon.

941 Almost half of the U.S. population lives in coastal regions.

942 The most common city name in the United States is "Franklin."

943 The world's largest dormant volcano, Haleakala, is located in Hawai'i.

944 75% of U.S. land that has a higher altitude than 10,000 feet is located in Colorado.

945 There is only one place in the U.S. where four states meet: the intersection of Colorado, Arizona, New Mexico, and Utah.

Nebraska's official state drink is Kool-Aid. 946

947 There is a cave in Missouri filled with $4 billion worth of milk fat for cheese and butter.

In Iowa, a "Snickers salad" is chopped up Snickers candy, green apples, and whipped topping. 948

949 Clark, South Dakota hosts a Mashed Potato Wrestling Contest.

The world's only Corn Palace is located in Mitchell, South Dakota. 950

951 The space between your eyebrows is called the glabella.

952 Over 17 million gallons of wine are produced in California every year.

953 In Russia, mail carriers carry revolvers.

954 In the 1930s, tomato ketchup was used as medicine.

955 The word "dude" was coined in the state of Wyoming at the Eaton Dude Ranch.

956 There are more Spanish speakers in the United States than in Spain.

957 The Hawaiian alphabet has only 12 letters. Almost half are vowels.

958 The only letter in the English alphabet that isn't in any U.S. state name is Q.

959 In 1922 at the Los Angeles County fair, one attraction demonstrated how to make toothpaste out of oranges.

960 In 1820 in New Jersey, tomatoes were put on trial at a courthouse to prove they weren't poisonous.

961 Rayne, Louisiana is the Frog Capital of the World.

962 Gueydan, Louisiana is the Duck Capital of America.

963 Michigan is known as the Wolverine State. However, there are no wolverines in Michigan anymore.

964 In South Dakota's Fountain Inn, horses are only allowed inside if they are wearing pants.

965 The biggest migratory elk herd in the U.S. is located in Montana.

966 In Georgia, it's illegal to keep a donkey in a bathtub.

967 Venice, Florida is the Shark Tooth Capital of the World.

968 In Wyoming, women are not legally allowed to drink while standing within 5 feet of a bar.

969 It's illegal to whistle underwater in West Virginia.

970 In West Virginia, it was once illegal to own a red or black flag.

971 The largest hand-planted forest in the world is in Nebraska.

972 Las Vegas, Nevada has more hotel rooms than anywhere else in the world.

973 The world's tallest water tower is located in New Jersey.

974 The amount of land used in the U.S. to cultivate corn is as big as all of Germany.

975 The largest helium well in the world is located in Amarillo, Texas.

976 New Mexico has more sheep and cattle than people.

977 There are annual duck races in Deming, New Mexico.

978 The state of Florida once named a hippo an honorary citizen.

979 The first railroad in the U.S. was 11 miles long. It was located in New York.

980 The first state to require cars to have license plates was New York.

981 The first traffic light in the United States was installed in Cleveland, Ohio in 1914.

982 The first city to use police cars was Akron, Ohio.

983 Until 1977, the U.S. had a presidential yacht.

984 The first school in the U.S. opened in 1696 in Maryland.

985 At the University of California, Berkeley, 16 elements on the periodic table were discovered.

986 Thomas Jefferson designed several buildings on the University of Virginia campus.

987 Hawai'i's Big Island has more scientific observatories than anywhere else in the world.

988 Americans spend more money on shoes and jewelry than they do on higher education.

989 Jupiter is bigger than all the other planets in our solar system combined.

990 Emus and kangaroos cannot walk backwards, and are on the Australian coat of arms for that reason.

991 There are 1 million ants for every human in the world.

992 One third of all cancers are sun related.

993 Wild dolphins call each other by name.

994 A dragonfly has a lifespan of 24 hours.

995 Giraffes have no vocal cords.

996 Eight of the ten largest statues in the world are of Buddhas.

997 Craving ice is a symptom of iron deficiency.

998 The olm salamander has a maximum lifespan of over 100 years.

999 Saudi Arabia is the largest country in the world without a river.

1000 Just 2% of the entire world's population is naturally blonde.

1001 Dora the Explorer's real name is Dora Márquez.

1002 Steve Jobs had a high school GPA of 2.65.

DID YOU KNOW?

THE FIRST WEBCAM EVER WATCHED A COFFEE POT.